EDGE
OF
MANHOOD

by THOMAS FALL

Illustrated by Henry C. Pitz

SCHOLASTIC BOOK SERVICES

NEW YORK • TORONTO • LONDON • AUCKLAND • SYDNEY • TOKYO

SHAWNEE WORDS
(Spelling according to English pronunciation)

AMI-A-QUA .... beaver
EL-E-NEY .... man
KA-AN-AH .... friend
KAW-QUA .... porcupine
KUH-KOOM-THEY-NAH ...... Our Grandmother
—Great Spirit
LA-LA-SO-WAW-KA .... instrument for
punishment
NI-QUE-THA .... my son
NO-TOB-OLEY .... war
POU-TA-LA .... skin for carrying bear oil
QUEG-A-WAI .... blanket
SA-COU-KA .... flintstone
SCOO-TEE .... fire
SCOU-TE-CA-GA .... steel for striking a flint
SEE-A-WAY .... horse
SKE-MO-TAH .... net woven by the Creator
SQUAW-THEE .... little
TEE-QUA .... gun
THEE-PEE .... river
THICK-O-WAY ...... board for carrying baby on
mother's back
THO-THEY-AW .... buffalo
WE-GI-WA* .... bark covered pole house
WIS-KE-LU-THA .... bird

*From which the word *wigwam* probably derived.

ISBN: 0-590-08617-0
Copyright © 1964 by Thomas Fall. This edition is published by Scholastic Book Services, a division of Scholastic Magazines, Inc., by arrangement with The Dial Press.

12 11 10 9 8 7 6 5 4   0 1 2/8

Contents

The Dream

THE BOY would always remember the last night of the journey with his family into the Indian Territory. They had camped along the bank of a river and because of the drizzling rain they slept under the wagon. The boy was lucky to be traveling in a wagon, for many of the Shawnee families moving south that winter had to walk.

His name was See-a-way, which in his Shawnee language meant horse. It was a shortened version of his full name which was Prancing-with-Spirit-on-the-Prairie.

He had the most curious and frightening dream that night. He dreamed he was making his way through a dark wood, alone, only to find himself suddenly surrounded by white men whose deathly pale faces loomed like horrible ghosts in the blackness. As the faces stared at him, they nodded forward, rhythmically, and he could hear muted noises accompanying the rhythms. The sounds seemed to say: *put-put put-put-put.*

His father touched his shoulder, shaking him gently to rouse him from the bad dream. He woke in a panic, terrified that the white men were reaching for him.

"Sh-h . . ." his father said in a low whisper. "Go back to sleep now, See-a-way, and dream of happier things. Try to dream about your manhood hunt. You will begin your endurance tests as soon as the spring planting is finished."

"Father, the white men were all around me—"

"Sh-h . . . we must not wake your mother and sister. They are tired from the long journey."

The boy lay as still as he could. The drizzle of rain was very light now, but he could hear it in the tall grass which surrounded the wagon in the edge of the blackjack copse beside the river. The air was cold and he snuggled deep into *queg-a-wai*, the word in his language for a coarse woolen blanket, wishing he could fall asleep instantly and dream of being roasty warm and dry somewhere before a great fire in a real house.

He had not lived in a house since he could remember, although he was told that he had been born in one in Kansas when his family had gone there to rejoin the Shawnee clan after they were driven out of Texas. He had always lived in a *we-gi-wa*—or out in the open when they were traveling, which was often. He hated rain at night, for then there was no moon or stars and he

had to sleep under the wagon, where he sometimes dreamed bad dreams.

He heard the strange sounds again. *Put-put
put-put-put.* Once more his father touched his
shoulder and whispered softly:

"It is only the wild turkey, See-a-way. Something disturbs him when he makes that sound in
the night."

"Maybe white men are creeping through the
woods along the river," he whispered back.

"No, my son, it is probably a wildcat, and the
turkeys warn each other."

"Maybe we could shoot a turkey for our food
tomorrow."

"There is no moon tonight, so we could not see
them, even if we tried."

"Are turkeys very hard to shoot?" he asked.

"Yes, they are hard to kill with an arrow or a
spear," his father said, still whispering, "but
easier with a gun. Perhaps you would like to
hunt a turkey for your manhood."

"I would!" he said aloud. "I will kill one and
roast it!"

"Sh-h . . ." his father said, patting his shoulder.

Up in Kansas, where they had been living,
there were not many wild turkeys. He had heard
that down here in the deep grass of the Indian
Territory turkeys could be found in flocks of a

3

thousand. Thoughts of actually having more turkey than he could eat sometimes made him burst into laughter, and when people asked what he was laughing about he would not tell them because he did not want to admit how hungry he was.

"When will we reach our new land?" he asked, once more lowering his voice to the barest whisper. He had asked this question frequently, for the journey had seemed endless. Of course, he knew the answer before his father told him, but he wanted to hear it again.

"Tomorrow, my son," his father replied, and it seemed almost too wonderful. "If the rain does not slow us down," he added, "we will camp tomorrow night at the site of our new home."

"Will we have a real house, Father?"

"Your mother will build a we-gi-wa for us at first," his father said. A *we-gi-wa* was a pole house, or lodge, made of hickory poles covered with slabs of elm bark or animal hides. "And later, my son, if all goes well for us, we will have a real house. If so, you will help me hew the logs and split the shakes for the roof and make the chinking."

"What *could* go wrong for us, Father?" he asked, feeling a sudden panic in his stomach. "Hasn't all the land between the North Fork and the South Fork of the big river been given to the

4

Shawnees for their new home?"

"Yes, it has."

"Isn't it to be our land as long as the grass grows and water runs downhill?"

"Yes, that is our promise from the white man."

"Did he not tell us the same thing when he drove us from Ohio to Texas? And again the same thing when he moved us up to Kansas?"

"But we are going to live in the Indian Territory this time, my son. It will be all right. All the Shawnees will have a place to live and plenty of room to plant corn and beans and pumpkins in the creek bottoms, where there are acorns and nuts for the hogs, lots of grass for the horses, and blackberries and persimmons for us to eat."

"I will help hew out great logs for a fine house," the boy said, "and if the white man sends his soldiers to make us move again, I will kill him!"

"Sh-h . . . go to sleep, now. Tomorrow we must travel many miles so that we can reach our new home. . . ."

Again the boy lay still, wide awake in the darkness, listening to the restless turkeys in the distant trees. He could hear rain drip from the wagon—spokes near his ear. From far across the river he could hear a cat owl's wail, making the night fairly shiver with its baleful *hoo hoo-hoo hoo hoo. . . .*

5

Endurance Tests

SEE-A-WAY had never seen a white man. Back in Kansas he might have gone many times to the trading posts with his father, but he had always stayed at home because he knew that white men were at the trading posts and he was afraid of them. He had always waited apprehensively for his father's return.

Entering the new place called Indian Territory, however, made him feel safe. And during the first joyous season he was there with his family the sky was always endlessly blue, with occasional large lazy white clouds—which only sometimes took the shape of white men before his eyes.

See-a-way's family established itself on the side of a knoll above a rushing creek. When the sap began to run in the elm trees, he helped his mother cut and pry off great slabs of bark, which were placed face down in many stacks with stones on top to straighten them as they dried. His older sister cut hickory poles which they tied

6

together into a rectangular framework with narrow strips of tough bark. They tied a ridge pole into tall forked poles at the front and back and center of the frame. Rafter poles reached down from the ridge to the sides. His mother climbed up to secure the great slabs of elm bark to the frame and within a few days the family was living in a new *we-gi-wa*.

See-a-way now felt even more secure. He knew that after a harvest of corn and pumpkins, and after trapping and stretching the hides of many animals for next winter's clothing, they might begin cutting logs for a real house. It did not seem possible to him that one boy could be so happy.

Many Shawnee families were already living here, and still others had come at the same time his family came. They helped each other clear patches of land for cultivation, and the boy asked his father when they could begin planting their seeds.

"After the Bread Dance of our people," his father explained. "The seeds will rot in the ground unless we give thanks to Kuh-koom-they-nah before we plant."

"And after we grow corn, we will always have bread to eat!" he said.

"Your mother will make meal and hominy and blue biscuit, and your sister will find pecans and walnuts and huckleberries and papaws and plums for us. You and I will hunt for deer and squirrel and quail and ducks and wild chickens after you have become a man—which may be soon," he added with a touch of mystery.

"And turkeys?" See-a-way asked, trembling with eagerness.

"Yes, my son." His father's voice now bore a teasing note. "Perhaps even before the Bread Dance you will begin your endurance tests."

"I feel very strong, Father!"

"Strong enough to begin right now?"

"Yes!"

"All right, See-a-way, my helpful son. . . . Do you remember where the large cottonwood tree hangs out over the creek, below the rocky ledge that comes down from the arroyo?"

"Yes!" the boy said. "The big limb reaches high above the rocks."

"Run, as fast as you can, and climb out on that limb. Then dive into the water. It is shallow below the limb, so you must dive far out or you may be killed on the rocks. Swim ashore and come back as fast you can run. I will see how long it takes, and decide if you are beginning to become a man. . . ."

See-a-way left so fast he scarcely heard his father finish the instructions.

He ran to the creek bank, then down to the tree

above the rocks formed by the arroyo. Quickly he pulled off his clothes. Because so few animal hides had been available that year, his mother had made him leggings from the sleeves of an old woolen hunting coat she had found somewhere, and he almost tore one of them in his hurry to get them off.

This was the first of many tests his father would give him before sending him out to hunt a wild turkey for his final proof of manhood, and he was eager to perform it well.

Indian boys were given manhood tests in order to eliminate the weak ones before they reached the age of responsibility. If he were reckless and let himself be killed, then it would save his people the danger of some day having to rely on an unsure leader who might get the entire tribe into trouble.

He climbed out on the high limb of the cotton-wood tree and looked down at the swirling water. The air was cold but it felt wonderful. He could see the slabs of stone below the surface, and far out from the limb the water was darker green, indicating that it was deeper there in a hole just downstream from the ledge.

He balanced himself on the limb for a moment; then, springing with all his might, he dived toward the hole.

He realized that he must have hurried his

dive, for he felt his right foot slip on the smooth bark of the cottonwood—just enough to lessen the power of his jump. As he sailed headfirst through the air he had a sickening feeling that he would not quite reach the deep pool.

He felt his face against the rocks. Pain stabbed at his cheek and shoulder. He had no control over his arms and legs—he was being swept along in the stream, and he knew he would drown if he did not get his head out of the water.

Then he realized that someone was helping him—undoubtedly his father. He felt a moment of terrible shame. He would rather have broken up on the rocks completely than face his father as a failure. A dead son was surely preferable to a son who had failed.

The next thing See-a-way remembered was lying in a bed of leaves, and looking up into the face of a stranger.

It was not his father who had saved him—it was a young man, older than himself. Although the air was cold and the stranger was soaking wet, he was not trembling. Whoever he was, he had attained his manhood. The boy knew that by the look on the young man's face, knew by the certainty of his manner . . . knew in the way that only a boy can know the exact difference between a man and a boy.

"My foot slipped when I dived into the water,"

he said. He tried to keep from shivering but he could not.

"I was watching you," the young man replied. "You are Shawnee, aren't you?"

The young man's words were in the Shawnee tongue but the boy knew from the way he pronounced them that he belonged to a different tribe.

"Yes, I am Shawnee. Thank you for saving my life . . . although I have failed my first endurance test. It would be just as well if I had died."

"Oh no," the young man told him quickly. "You misunderstand. Manhood means to be relied upon to survive. There is nothing dishonorable about being softer than a stone! There is nothing dishonorable about making a mistake, unless it is repeated. Your obligation is to try again, and be successful."

The boy stared up at the young man, respecting him.

"Are you from the Kickapoo?" he asked.

"No. I am a Pottawatomie."

"Why are you here on our land? The Kickapoo and the Iowa are near us on the Creek reservation, but I did not know the Pottawatomie were here."

The young man's face grew troubled.

"We were given the land west of the Creeks—

between the North Fork and the South Fork of the big river."

"But so were we!" cried the boy. "The Shawnees have been given this land!"

"I know, I know," said the young man sternly. "I heard about it today from my people. The white man has given the same land to both tribes. Now we must fight each other for it. We can't fight the white man, he is too strong."

"If we must fight each other, then why did you save my life?" the boy asked, closely watching the strong Pottawatomie face before him.

"I would not let a boy die. Perhaps if you had been a man I would not have helped you." The young man smiled suddenly. "Anyway," he said, "I did not know you were a Shawnee. You were without clothes, climbing out on a tree limb. I wondered if some boy had been eating the loco weed. Then I saw your clothes at the base of the tree, so I knew you were not a naked Indian from the plains, even though you were naked when I saw you."

They both laughed, despite the seriousness of the situation. For they both realized that white men made no distinction between the Indians of the east who wore clothes and planted crops for a living, and the naked Indians of the western plains who were nomadic, lived by hunting, and wore only blankets during the winter and scarcely anything but breechclouts and perhaps a few feathers when the weather was warm.

"Do you really think," asked the boy, "that my people and yours will have to fight for the land between the two rivers? Isn't there enough land for both tribes?"

"No," said the young man. His eyes became sullen. "We will starve if both our tribes try to live here together. I have been told that we must drive the Shawnee out as soon as possible. Therefore, I cannot be friends with you. You are not yet a man, anyway." From the look in his eyes he could have become murderous then and there. The boy realized that no doubt he too had been dreaming of having all he could eat and a safe place to live.

"Where do you live?" See-a-way asked.

"Above the horseshoe bend in the big river. Above the muddy bottomland."

"Perhaps, if we joined together to fight the white man—"

"We would all die if we tried. No wonder you are still a boy if you don't know that. You must be stupid like the sheep and the cow."

Silently the boy put on his clothes. The young man watched closely.

"Did you Shawnees come down here from Kansas?"

14

"Yes."

"What is your name?"

"See-a-way," said the boy. "It means horse."

The young man nodded and told his own Pottawatomie name and said, "In your language it means Blue Eagle. Well, See-a-way, it is too bad that we must fight each other."

"Are you *sure* we must?" the boy asked, his pulse pounding.

"Yes," said Blue Eagle in a voice that made the boy tremble. "But you are safe from me until you have passed your manhood tests. Then, if your people are still on our land, I may one day have to kill you. . . ."

The young man turned abruptly and strode to his pony, hobbled beside a greasewood tree. And with the easiest spring the boy had ever seen, Blue Eagle hopped upon his pony and rode toward the horseshoe bend in the big river.

The Bread Dance

HIS FATHER pretended not to notice his bruised face. He merely mentioned that he had taken quite a while to complete his first test. See-a-way was afraid he would not be given another test very soon. But his father surprised him with two more tests before the Bread Dance. One was to see how long he could stand on his left foot on a log that crossed the creek near their *we-gi-wa*. He stood on the log until he collapsed from dizziness and fell into the water and he had no idea whether or not he had passed the test. It would not be known for certain if he had passed anything until he was sent on his actual manhood hunt. The manhood hunt was never directed until a satisfactory number of endurance tests had been successfully completed.

The third test was to stick a *kaw-qua* quill into his hand and leave it there all day, to be cut out with a sharp knife that night. *Kaw-qua* meant porcupine. The barbs on the quill made it go deeper the longer it stayed in the flesh.

That night See-a-way stood quietly while his

father cut out the quill. It was very painful, but the boy stood completely motionless. As he cut, his father told him that a school for Indian children was going to be built by a Quaker missionary named Sparkman who had come into the Indian country. Suddenly, the boy was very near tears, but it had nothing to do with the physical pain. The idea of a school was far more painful.

"Aren't Quakers white men?" he asked, standing before his father, rigid as a frozen squirrel skin.

"Yes, but they are good white men, See-a-way. You must learn that all white men are not bad."

"They can't be good if they are white, can they?" cried the boy.

His father's grip tightened on his wrist as he worked with the knife. He did not answer the question, and the boy knew he did not want it asked again.

At last his father pulled out the quill and examined it on the end of the knife blade. He said, "Many of the Kickapoo and Iowa children will be going to the school. It will be directed by the Sac and Fox agency, which has charge of all the reservations near us. If you learn to read and write the white man's language, my son, as well as our own, you will be able to help our people some day."

"I will kill them," the boy said under his breath, for he knew that his father must not hear him display temper. He could tell that his father was proud of the way he had stood for the *kaw-qua* quill to be cut out, and he did not want to set back his manhood progress by revealing how desperately he hated white men and their ways.

"*I will kill them.* I will not go to their school," his mind kept saying over and over, so loud in his ear that he did not hear what his father was telling him. All he knew was that his father continued to speak of the advantages of learning to read and write at the Quaker missionary's school....

See-a-way did not mention to his family that he had met a young Pottawatomie brave named Blue Eagle, but he heard much talk about the unwanted presence of Pottawatomie on the land between the rivers. It might be terrible for him to think of any enemy as a friend, yet he could not forget that Blue Eagle had saved his life. Above all, he did not want to be punished with the *la-la-so-waw-ka*—an instrument made by pushing long thorns through a board so that the sharp points stuck out on the other side. It tore the flesh of the leg or thigh of anyone punished with it, and it was never used on children unless their crime was extremely serious. He had no idea how serious it was to be friends with an enemy. Perhaps to conceal the fact that a Pottawatomie had saved his life was also a crime—and he was afraid that no matter what he did, he would deserve to be raked with the dreaded *la-la-so-waw-ka*.

Because he had not yet reached his manhood, such things as trouble with the Pottawatomie were never openly discussed in his presence. But he heard bits of conversation, and he saw the looks on all the faces. He did not dare ask questions, but wondered if the Shawnees outnumbered the Pottawatomie, in case of a showdown war. Most of all, in spite of Blue Eagle's explanation, he wondered why Indians must fight each other instead of the white man.

If there were not enough Pottawatomie and Shawnee combined to kill the white men, surely they could persuade the Iowa and the Kickapoo and the Creek and maybe even the great Cherokee and Seminole tribes to join them, and chase the white men back across the water to wherever they came from.

He longed for the day he would reach his manhood so he could suggest in council a mass warfare of all Indians everywhere against the white man. Some day perhaps he would be a great chief, like their departed Shawnee leader,

Tecumseh, but he would never make the mistake of joining the white men in their wars against one another, as Tecumseh had done when he led the Shawnees to the British during a great war. He would simply have let the white people kill each other off, leaving the land to the Indians who had always used it.

As the full moon of April approached, plans for the first Bread Dance on the new reservation began, and for a while their problems gave way to the joy of preparation.

See-a-way watched and often helped as the women and girls gathered great piles of firewood at the site of the dance ground. He was growing too proud to do women's work, but the excitement of the celebration prodded him. Logs were arranged around the dancing area for seats, and soon the night was bright with bonfires. The twelve official Bread Dance hunters had left three days before the moon was full. As the bonfires burned brightly and the drums began to sound, the boy eagerly waited with his family for the return of the hunters.

When they finally arrived with deer, antelope, wild turkey and many quail, the Shawnees gave a loud, hungry cheer. The twelve cooking women, appointed by the chief to cook for the Bread

Dance, received the game the hunters had killed and then moved in a slow circle around the fires, dancing a solemn song of thanks to the sound of drums.

Suddenly Ami-a-qua, the oldest man of the clan, made his way feebly to the center of the gathering and held up his hands.

"What is he going to do?" the boy whispered to his father. He knew the answer, of course, but he enjoyed having his father tell him. Explanations of such things always brought a sound of reverence into his father's voice that moved the boy deeply.

"He will thank Our Grandmother for the game we have to eat, and ask for good feeling and good health among our people."

His people believed that Kuh-koom-they-nah, which was the Shawnee way of saying "Our Grandmother," sat in the sky all day and all night in her large rocking chair, silently rocking and weaving a great net, *Ske-mo-tah,* which would some day be lowered to earth to gather up all the Shawnees who had proved worthy of life everlasting. The rest of the world, they believed, would then come to an end. That was some consolation to See-a-way. It took care of the white man nicely—for no white man would ever be lifted into the sky in a *Ske-mo-tah!*

He glanced upward, even though it was night, to see if he could find the hole in the sky from which Our Grandmother watched everything that was done on earth. She was a huge, very old woman, he knew, with long gray hair. Babies were sometimes born with one of her gray hairs in their heads, and if such a thing happened to a boy his chance of becoming a chief was very good.

See-a-way did not think he had been born with a gray hair, but nobody had ever mentioned it to him.

"Did Kuh-koom-they-nah really provide the deer and the turkeys, Father?"

"Yes, my son, Kuh-koom-they-nah provides everything we have," the boy's father told him.

"My mother provided our *we-gi-wa*," he said stubbornly.

"But Our Grandmother provided the hickory poles and the elm bark."

"Why does old Ami-a-qua pray for us, Father?"

"Because he is the oldest and wisest man in our clan."

"Will you ever be wise enough to pray for us?"

"Some day, perhaps—if I live long enough, and if our chief should select me."

"How does our chief know if a person is wise enough to pray?" the boy asked.

"If a person is honest and unafraid and learns to keep his temper during a crisis," his father said simply, "he may be qualified to pray."

The boy felt suddenly uneasy. He did not know how it would be possible ever to keep one's temper during a crisis and plan a war at the same time!

"When we lived in Kansas," he asked, "did old Ami-a-qua pray that Our Grandmother would send us here to live?"

"No, my son, I don't think he did."

"Because the white man sent us here to live, didn't he? Why doesn't Ami-a-qua pray to the white man for the deer and turkeys and corn and berries—?"

"See-a-way, my son! You must gentle your

voice, and also your heart," his father said, putting an arm around the boy's shoulder.

"Does Kuh-koom-they-nah always live above the clouds where she watches all the time through a hole in the sky?"

"Yes, She does."

"Does She also watch the white man?"

"You must not ask so many questions," his father said.

"How large are the white men, Father?" the boy persisted. "Are they very large and strong?"

"Some of them are quite large."

"Larger even than the Cherokee and the Creek?"

"Some of them are, but not all of them."

"Have you seen very many white men, Father?"

"I have seen several. Most of them are no larger than we are."

"Are they very white?"

"Yes, they are like ghosts."

"Are they frightening, Father?"

"No. Many of them are evil, but they are not frightening."

"Then why do we always have to go where they send us to live?"

"Hush, now... Ami-a-qua is about to speak to us."

"I would like to see a white man some time," said the boy grimly, "after I have passed my manhood tests, and have shot a wild turkey through the heart with my longbow!"

His father's arm pulled him tightly to warn him that he was much too agitated.

They stood quietly before the ring of bonfires as Ami-a-qua began to speak.

Stolen Horses

OLD AMI-A-QUA told them during the prayer ceremony that it was wrong to harm their neighbors, for they would only harm themselves if they did. The Shawnee people grew even more silent.

See-a-way knew they were all thinking of the Pottawatomie. But how could they quarrel if it was wrong to harm one another?

They listened tensely as Ami-a-qua told them that, in return for the miracle of life which Kuh-koom-they-nah would put into their seeds, they must be truthful and have respect for each other. That was the payment Kuh-koom-they-nah always required.

Then, as the boy listened, Ami-a-qua asked blessings from the Pumpkin Person, the Corn Person, the Summer Man, the Water Person, and the Tree Man. And he asked for pity from the Cyclone Man, the North Wind Person, and the Thunderers.

Then the old man lifted his wrinkled hands

even higher and warned his people never, never to speak the white man's language.

The boy's heart leaped. He looked at his father and said, "Did you hear? Did you, Father? That means I cannot go to the Quaker's school—"

"Sh-h...Ami-a-qua is still talking...."

The boy waited with impatience until Ami-a-qua finished. Then he pursued the subject.

"If he is the wisest elder of our people, Father, how can we disobey him?"

"Being the wisest elder does not necessarily mean that he is always right," his father said.

"I do not understand—"

"You do not wish to understand, my son. Ami-a-qua's wisdom is of the old order. The desire to understand new and difficult problems is as much a part of reaching manhood as passing the physical tests. It is more important for the young than for the old."

"But...can Ami-a-qua be wrong about this, Father—and yet be wise enough to pray for us? Suppose he should ask Kuh-koom-they-nah for the wrong things?"

"Our Grandmother would not answer a prayer that would be bad for us. Our prayers reflect the questions in our hearts, even if the answers we decide on are wrong. Our Grandmother judges us only by our questions."

"Doesn't Kuh-koom-they-nah give us the answers to the things we ask?"

"We are never given any answers at all. Kuh-koom-they-nah only gives us the will to find the best answers we can. Do not fret, my son. You will understand in due time, and then you will have achieved your manhood...."

After the Bread Dance ceremony the boy stood alone in the fire shadows and watched the Frolic Dance begin. It occurred to him that if he could understand enough to achieve his manhood before the school was built, then he would not have to go to it.

As he thought about these things, he felt his father's arm on his shoulder again.

"See-a-way, it is now time to have some fun. The solemn prayers are finished, and you should dance in the circle around the fires."

"Is it really wrong to harm our neighbors, Father?" asked the boy. "Does old Ami-a-qua know about the Pottawatomie on our land—?"

"My son! You are trying to have thoughts too old for your years. After your manhood I will talk to you about these things."

His father's dark eyes glistened in the light from the fires and the boy cringed under the disapproving gaze.

"If you will watch your sister closely," his

father said, "I think before the Frolic Dance is over you may see something very interesting...."

The boy turned toward the fires.

His sister danced in the wide circle of girls and women, and when she came to a brave she wished to dance with, he saw what his father had meant. She stood behind Wis-ke-lu-tha, whose Shawnee name meant bird. And she did not offer him her handkerchief to hold onto as they danced together. She offered him her bare hand. That meant she would consent to marry him if he cared for her. And the boy could tell that she was being accepted. He was sure she knew she would be before she stood behind Wis-ke-lu-tha, but he did not know how she knew. One thing was certain; soon they would be living in a *we-gi-wa* of their own. To dance without a handkerchief between their hands made them husband and wife.

Everyone smiled and nodded happily. The boy watched, admiring Wis-ke-lu-tha because of his broad shoulders and his great strength. And although it was difficult to understand why such a fine man should be interested in his sister, it would be a proud thing to have Wis-ke-lu-tha in the family. For it was the custom among Shawnees for the man to become part of the woman's family, and See-a-way looked at his sister with newly discovered esteem.

The feeling of joy was suddenly shattered, however, as one of the braves who had been on pasture patrol burst swiftly into the dancing grounds on a pony, shouting at the top of his voice.

"The Pottawatomie! They have stolen all our horses! They have broken our fences and scattered our hogs!"

This could only have happened because his people had left so few braves on patrol during the Bread Dance. It was especially terrible for the Pottawatomie to take advantage of a sacred ceremonial night to steal horses!

"My son!" his father said to him. "Go home with your mother and sister. Do not leave them!" That was all he said. He ran to Wis-ke-lu-tha, and together they hurried from the dancing grounds with the other men to pursue the thieves. See-a-way would have given anything if his manhood tests had been completed so that he might have gone with them.

Horses and cattle were the Shawnee's most valuable possessions and were kept in a single community herd which the braves took turn patrolling. They also kept riding ponies, calves and hogs.

See-a-way's mother had been given two calves by drovers whose herds had passed on one of the cattle trails that crossed the Indian Territory from Texas to the northern markets. He had resented his mother's taking anything from the white men, but his father said she should. The drovers always killed or gave away any calves that were born along the way, for keeping them only slowed down the trail herds.

Therefore, the boy knew, it was possible in time for the Shawnee women to accumulate cattle. But until the calves grew up, the only things they had to trade for cash were horses.

The riding ponies, of course, were kept in individual pens, or hobbled near their owners' homes. The hogs, which the Shawnees had brought from Kansas, were all kept together near the creek valley in a large hog pasture, which had been fenced in even before the women built the *we-gi-was*. Now they discovered that the hogs, so essential for food, had been scattered up and down the long valley by the marauding Pottawatomie!

The boy lay in his bed and thought about the tragedy that had befallen even before the first planting in the new land. His bed, in one corner of the *we-gi-wa,* consisted of four poles laid out on the ground to form a rectangle. It was filled with evergreen boughs and leaves, upon which he curled up in his *queg-a-wai* to sleep.

But he slept very little that night. When he did, he dreamed of having to fight with Blue Eagle. He still could think of a person who had saved his life only as a friend, and he kept waking up in a cold sweat. In one of his dreams Blue Eagle was trying to drown him in a river, saying that it had been a foolish mistake to save the life of a Shawnee boy who was more stupid than sheep and cows. But he also said to See-a-way in the dream: "I will let you out of the water if you will promise to shoot a white man instead of a wild turkey for your manhood hunt...."

The boy woke in excitement. That was surely the most splendid idea he had ever had in his life, even if Blue Eagle did suggest it in a dream.

But he knew that he could not ask his father to assign him a white man instead of a wild turkey. And he wondered if he could ever understand his father's attitude, for he knew that in the past his people had killed many white men as the tribe was being pushed thousands of miles into one new land after another.

His father and Wis-ke-lu-tha did not come home until the next afternoon. The horses had been traced, they said, through the tall grass leading from the horse pasture to a small river. Apparently the Pottawatomie had driven the horses down the river for some distance and then out through the woods onto a well-used cattle trail.

The Shawnees had followed the cattle trail all morning until they caught up with a trail herd and recognized their horses in the remuda. But the trail boss, who was of course a white man, said he had purchased the horses from Indians. He did not know which Indians, he said, because he could not tell one Indian from another. He then pulled out his guns and the Shawnee, the rightful owners of the horses, were forced to run for their lives.

For two or three days See-a-way wandered around alone, stunned by the tragedy, refusing to talk to anybody. His father watched him silently. He felt that his father expected something special of him, but he did not know what. He kept hoping to be given his next endurance test. But endurance tests were given when you were considered worthy, not merely because you were impatient for them.

Soon he learned that plans for retaliation against the Pottawatomie were under way among his people. He listened very carefully to the talk. Always he had to pretend not to be listening, however, or the men would not have spoken in his presence. He spent as much time as he could at his sister's *we-gi-wa,* for Wis-ke-lu-

34

tha was helping his father make the plans for revenge, which would be presented to their chief for approval. For a wedding present his sister had been given a coal oil lamp by her husband, which provided the boy with an excuse for being there. It was the first oil lamp he had ever seen and everyone knew how fascinated he was by it. He would sit and stare at the lamp for hours— always listening.

The plan was for the Shawnees to steal the Pottawatomie horses. Scouting patrols of Shawnee braves were sent for miles down the cattle trail and into the vicinity of all the Indian agencies and trading posts in search of buyers for the Pottawatomie horses. And other scouts were sent to locate them.

The boy at last heard Wis-ke-lu-tha say bitterly to his father: "Our chief has approved the plan. He does not care if this means *no-tob-oley!*"

No-tob-oley was war.

A Surprise Meeting

SEE-A-WAY had not seen Blue Eagle since the young Pottawatomie pulled him from the creek. He remembered that Blue Eagle lived above the muddy bottomland near the horseshoe bend of the big river, and despite his hatred of the Pottawatomie, he could not help thinking of Blue Eagle as a friend.

The only reason he hesitated to go above the horseshoe bend, however, was fear that he might unwittingly betray his own people by warning the Pottawatomie that the horses would soon be stolen.

The day he actually went, he did not intend to. He had been practicing with his longbow, shooting at rabbits and a few wild chickens. He had only been able to kill one of each, but the practice made his arm stronger and his aim straighter all the time.

He realized that without thinking he had wandered near the big horseshoe. It was a bright,

hot morning, with no clouds to cool the sky. Heat
shimmers were rising from the dampness in the
muddy bottomland and the hot smell of growing
grass was sweet in his nostrils. He paused near a
willow thicket, deciding that he must not go any
farther, when suddenly Blue Eagle, hands on
hips, stepped out from behind a huge tree in front
of him. The boy was so startled that his heart
beat wildly.

"Hello, See-a-way," Blue Eagle said in Shawnee.

"Hello," said the boy, staring at him. He did
not look quite the same.

"Let me show you how to shoot a longbow. I

hope you are not still stupid like the sheep." He reached out and took the longbow from See-a-way's hand.

The boy then gave him arrows and watched in amazement as he split every twig he aimed at, and pierced every leaf exactly in the middle.

As they gathered the arrows, Blue Eagle said, "Are you here to spy on my people, See-a-way? Is that your new endurance test? If so, you can see now that you are not very safe."

"I am not spying," the boy told him. "I am practicing for my manhood hunt, nothing else."

"I can see that you are not getting to be smart and sly like the wolf or the fox. If your people knew you were here, at a time like this when we may go to war against each other, they would punish you. If anyone else had found you here, you might have been killed. You are beginning to look like a man, but you do not act like one."

"Why must we fight each other?" the boy asked. "Why don't we join together and fight the white man?"

Blue Eagle shrugged impatiently.

"It is very simple, See-a-way. Our people, for generations that go back to our grandfathers and even to their grandfathers, have been fighting the white man. But always the white men have won. Always they have pushed us wherever they wanted us to go. It is too late now. If we had killed them as fast as they got off their ships when they first landed on our continent, we might have been able to wipe them out. But they fooled us with gifts and we let them get a foothold. Now they can't be stopped. They call us filthy murdering animals while their governments defraud us and their armies take away our lands. We can only try to learn their ways and fight them with words instead of weapons. But you are probably too young to understand."

"Do you mean we should learn to speak their language?" the boy asked, horrified.

"Yes. I am going to school when the new Quaker mission is built near the agency."

"*You are?*"

The boy was dumbfounded. Since Blue Eagle had achieved manhood, he did not have to go to school unless he wanted to.

"I will *never* go to the school!" the boy said loudly.

Blue Eagle smiled a thin, sarcastic smile. His teeth had been sharpened with a file, and the boy realized that was what had made him seem different. His father would not let him sharpen his own teeth.

"See-a-way," said Blue Eagle, "you are still more stupid even than the sheep and the cow. I don't know why I bothered to save your life. You should have been born a naked Indian of the plains, so you could run around in a breechclout and do war dances and raid the white people all your life. The poor Plains Indians will be wiped out completely if they do not realize that they must learn the white man's way."

The boy was so furious at this that he could not think of anything that would make sense. So he said something foolish—and very dangerous. He said bitterly, "Why did your people steal our horses, Blue Eagle? You know it is not right to steal other people's—!"

He did not finish. Blue Eagle stepped toward him in a flash, grabbed his wrist, jerked him around over an outstretched foot and threw him to the ground. He put his foot on the boy's chest, and his rawhide moccasin smeared mud on the boy's homespun shirt.

"See-a-way," he said in a low voice that seemed to quiver with contempt, "I am going to let you up now and I hope I never have to throw you to the ground again."

Then he pointed in the direction from which the boy had come. And See-a-way knew he was meant to go that way in a hurry.

He picked up the rabbit and the wild chicken he had killed and walked toward his own home.

He did not hunt any more that day.

Nor was he ashamed that Blue Eagle had put him to the ground. If anything, Blue Eagle should be ashamed for doing it to a boy who had not yet reached manhood. A Shawnee brave would never have done that to any Indian boy— unless the boy's people were at war with the Shawnees.

For days See-a-way could not get out of his mind what Blue Eagle had said about going to school. Make friends with the white man and learn his terrible language? The idea of such a thing made him dizzy.

The knowledge that his grandfathers and their grandfathers had always fought the white men as they retreated westward into strange lands played on his fevered mind. Now most of the surviving Indian tribes were on reservations, crowded together on each other's lands, super- vised by agents and guarded by soldiers. Nearby, hunting along the same streams and plowing the same hillsides and valleys, were Sac and Fox, Kickapoo and Iowa, Creek and Seminole. And the boy knew he had recently traveled with his family through an area where Tonkawa and Ponca, Pawnee, Oto, Missouria, Osage and Kaw were cramped together, hunting and planting their corn as best they could. To the west, many wild Plains Indians had been herded onto reservations—Wichita and Caddo, Cheyenne and Arapaho, Kiowa, Comanche, and Apache. Up north, Peoria, Modoc, Wyandotte and Seneca had been driven into one corner of the lands the Cherokee were supposed to have had for their own as long as water ran downhill.

And he had heard that railroads were now under construction, headed toward them with huge steam engines puffing black smoke into the air, bringing more and more white men to crowd the Indians still closer together.

Thinking about it, the boy decided he would not mind at all being a savage Indian of the plains. At least he would then be free to kill the white man.

It was to him a shameful thing that Blue Eagle, already a brave with wonderfully sharpened teeth and the right to use his expert longbow in any way he chose, should talk of going to a Quaker school where he could learn the white man's terrible tongue.

See-a-way would rather sharpen his teeth, put on a breechclout, paint his face, and go on the warpath any day!

The Cattle Trail

THE SHAWNEE scouting parties returned with news that a horse buyer would be coming that way before the next full moon.

The Pottawatomie horses had been found, well hidden in the valley of a small stream that led toward the big river. A split-rail fence had been built across its mouth, which faced the river. Pottawatomie braves patrolled the hills on both sides of the valley. They also patrolled a line on the wide, high-grassed plateau at the opposite end. But there were no patrols at the mouth of the horse pasture because the fence would keep the horses from following the stream down toward the river.

The plan was for the Shawnees to encircle the pasture quietly, then ride in on their ponies, whooping and hollering, driving the horses downhill toward the rail fence. Shawnee men would have dismantled enough of the fence to let the horses through. The braves would stay behind to fight the Pottawatomie patrols, and older men would herd the horses several miles toward the cattle trail where the buyers would be waiting. This would be done during the daytime because the Pottawatomie would be more surprised by a raid in broad daylight than at night.

The boy had heard about all this as he had pretended not to be listening to the men. He was very proud of his father for thinking of a plan that their chief would approve, and he wished he could see the look on Blue Eagle's face when the Pottawatomie horses were stolen from under their very eyes.

It was not easy to wait for the time when the plan would be put into action. Every night he watched as the moon moved from its last quarter toward the first. During the days he practiced for his endurance tests. At night he stared at his sister's coal oil lamp and listened.

Already his sister was making a *thick-o-way*—a board, artistically decorated, to which a baby would be strapped when it was carried on its mother's back. He could not look at it without reaching up to feel the fine flat spot on the back of his own head. A baby boy was always bound to the *thick-o-way* so that a flat place would be formed on the back of his head, against which a banded head plate would fit for holding a feather when he reached his manhood and became a brave.

Now, at night, he watched the moon go through its first quarter toward the full, and during the daytime he practiced with his longbow. One day, when he had crossed the river and the cattle trail chasing a covey of quail he had flushed out of a wild plum brake, he saw in the distance a large wagon loaded with what looked like newly cut oak logs traveling in the direction of the Sac and Fox agency. As he watched, a second wagonload came into view.

When See-a-way told his father what he had seen, his father said, with speculative eyes, "Those were probably Friend Sparkman's logs for the mission school, See-a-way."

The boy looked down at the ground and did not answer. An eagle, circling overhead, cast its shadow before them. They both knew that it was not a good omen. They looked at each other once more.

"Have you been thinking about the school, my son?"

"Yes, Father, I have."

The boy was sure that the bird overhead was warning him, and that the strange feeling he had had for days was a premonition as well. Clearly, he should stay away from the school. He glanced back into the sky, to make his father conscious of the ominous bird again.

"I won't ask whether you have reached a decision," his father said.

Which meant, of course, that he did not care what decision his son might reach. Nor was he going to pay heed to a bad omen. His mind was made up and the boy knew it. See-a-way would join the other Indian children and attend the hated school whether he liked it or not.

But telling him this by implication was his father's way of letting him save face. That he could let the boy save face suggested that he considered his son worthy—and See-a-way felt comforted to know that he might soon be given another endurance test.

But still, the idea of having to go to the white man's school made the warm summer air seem cold against his face.

It occurred to him that if he had gone closer to the wagonloads of logs, he might have had his first look at a white man. He would not have dreamed of doing so at the time, but now he was sorry he hadn't.

However, if he stationed himself at a certain spot on the cattle trail, where the horse buyer was going to wait for the Pottawatomie horses, he could see a white man there.

When the day of the raid finally came, the boy waited until the men and braves had silently ridden away in different directions on their ponies. Then he slipped from his *we-gi-wa* and ran as fast as he could, cutting across the high-grass valley, then down through the blackjack thickets to the creek. He followed the creek to the river, then ran up the bank toward the cattle trail.

He walked slowly up the trail to an arroyo where all the stone outcroppings in the eroded red earth seemed to have been struck in anger by the Thunderers. From here he could sit out of sight and wait for his first glimpse of a white man.

He waited a very long time before he heard anything. Then the sound of bawling cows reached him from far down the trail, in the opposite direction from which he expected to see the horse buyer approach.

It looked as if a trail herd of cattle from Texas was crossing the Shawnee land. The cattle stretched out for a mile in the low flat grassland below the boy's vantage point on the side of the arroyo. Armed cowboys rode on either side of the herd, and a large remuda and wagons followed in the rear.

Suddenly the boy heard pounding hooves to

the west of the trail. That should be his people coming with the Pottawatomie horses. He realized that the horse buyer had not arrived, and wondered for a moment whether the plan had been changed.

Then the terrible thing happened.

The cowboys thought the approaching Shawnees were trying to stampede their cattle, and they fired into their midst even as the stolen Pottawatomie horses plunged into the trail herd. The boy saw his father fall off a pony. The cowboys were yelling and the Shawnees were yelling. The boy's heart was wild as he ran down the red clay embankment, jumped over the rocks and raced to where his father lay on the grass.

He reached his father and knelt beside him. He took his father's head into his lap.

"*Ni que-tha...*" was all his father could say.

The boy looked up at the stampeding cattle, now swirling in a mad run toward the east, up through the ravine of the red arroyo. The cowboys were trying to turn them back toward the trail. The other Shawnees were trying to round up the stolen horses, many of which had become so frightened by the stampede that they galloped like thunder up the trail to the north.

The boy looked down at his father whose eyes were now closed. For some strange reason he realized, as he looked at his father's still form, that for all this he had not yet seen a white man.

"Father..." he said.

But his father did not answer, and he knew why the eagle had circled a bad omen overhead that day. It was because his father was going to die, and he had thought it was to warn him not to go to the school.

A Strange Indian

OLD AMI-A-QUA, who had been selected to pray at the Bread Dance, was chosen to speak at the funeral of the boy's father. It therefore became Ami-a-qua's duty to pass out the sacred tobacco to the close friends of the family who came to mourn.

The *we-gi-wa* of See-a-way's parents was located on a gently sloping green hillside facing the morning sun, and the grave was dug by Wis-ke-lu-tha near the top of the knoll behind it. The boy watched as Ami-a-qua stood below the grave site, holding out a buckskin pouch filled with tobacco which had been ceremoniously blessed to protect his father's grave from evil influences. As the family friends marched in a line from the *we-gi-wa* up the winding path to the grave site, each would dip into Ami-a-qua's pouch and take out a pinch of the tobacco, holding it until he passed by the head of the grave. Then he would kneel for a moment and drop the

tobacco into the grave as he thought of the boy's
father.

When all the mourners had passed the grave
and returned to the *we-gi-wa* to wait, old Ami-a-
qua went alone to the grave and knelt before it.
He softly called to the boy's father several times,
pausing long enough finally for the departing
spirit to hear him. Then he said:

"Dear Brother, do not let the sorrow of your
family distract you from this journey to the
happy world above the sky. It is Our Grandmother's wish that all Her children come to Her
with untroubled minds and brave hearts."

Ami-a-qua then dropped his own pinch of sacred tobacco into the grave before he continued
speaking:

"Our Grandmother wishes me to tell you that
Her goodness will heal the sorrow of your loved
ones, and to remind you that their love for you
will still be with them when they meet you again
at Our Grandmother's side."

Ami-a-qua rose from the grave and walked
slowly back down the path to the *we-gi-wa*. As
Wis-ke-lu-tha and his friends went up to fill the
grave with dirt, old Ami-a-qua told everyone
stories about the brave adventures of the Shawnee people in the past. So gradually that the boy
hardly noticed it, the mood of the stories shifted

from serious to humorous. It was Ami-a-qua's duty to make everyone laugh if he could and thereby recover as quickly as possible from sorrow.

Soon everyone felt in a happier mood, and the women began cleaning up. Inside the *we-gi-wa* they stretched out all the blankets and clothing on rafter poles and they stacked all the pots into neat piles on the hearth. They swept the dirt floor clean of footprints, and then went out and swept the yard. All this time the boy watched his mother sitting quietly in one corner of the *we-gi-wa*. From time to time his sister or some of his mother's friends bathed her face with a cloth dipped into cool herb water. His mother was not required to end her grieving until the following day.

Several of the closest family friends stayed for four days after the funeral, never letting anyone think about grief for a moment. At the end of the four days they all took baths and washed their clothes and swept the yards again. For this was the day the boy's mother would select her new husband, and everything must be in good order. The boy watched his mother closely, wondering whom she would choose.

Ami-a-qua came inside and spoke to her: "Your departed husband, who now resides peacefully with Kuh-koom-they-nah, was a very good man, my sister. He hunted the deer and antelope and even the buffalo, and he hunted all the birds and all the small game, providing meat for food, skins for clothing, and teeth for beads and ornaments. He cherished you and the children you gave him. He knows that it is now your duty to choose a new husband for your household—a new father for your son who is approaching manhood. My sister, whom do you choose?"

The boy's mother did not hesitate. She chose Tho-they-aw El-e-ney—Buffalo Man.

Everyone smiled and departed, leaving the mother and Buffalo Man together in her *we-gi-wa*. They were now married, and See-a-way had a new father to give him his endurance tests.

His sister and Wis-ke-lu-tha took him to live with them for a few days. They sang songs together and sometimes, at night by the light of the wonderful oil lamp, they told stories.

During the ceremony and the four days of mourning and recovery from his father's death, the boy noticed that a certain stranger came often and stood near them. The stranger's skin was the color of old rawhide, and his face was wrinkled and creased from the sun although he wore a black hat with a wide brim to protect his eyes. His clothing was not like anything the boy had ever seen. He wore no leggings, but long black homespun pants and coat. Instead of moccasins he wore heavy leather shoes, which were quite shiny. Wis-ke-lu-tha had said that shoes like them could be bought at the trading post near the agency if one had a lot of money—so this man must be rich.

He spoke to everyone in the friendliest way and sounded like a Shawnee, but something was different. See-a-way decided that the stranger might be a member of the tribe that was separated from the main group back in Ohio when his people were still fighting the white man.

Each day during the mourning for his father, he would watch this strange Indian and listen when he could to everything the man said. The Shawnee seemed to hold the man in esteem, and therefore the boy longed to be noticed.

On the fourth day, while Ami-a-qua was inside the *we-gi-wa* with his mother, the strange tall Indian in the black hat came over and put his arm around the boy's shoulder much as his own father had done so often.

"You must be young See-a-way," the strange Indian said. A quiver of pride went through the boy to have been noticed at last.

56

"Yes, I am," he said excitedly. "Who are you, sir? I have not seen you before, but you must have been my father's friend."

He should not have asked such a question. It was a boy's place to answer only what was asked him. But in this instance curiosity was too great.

"I am your friend, too," the stranger said. "I am a friend of all your people."

The stranger's words were perfect—much better, in fact, than Blue Eagle's Shawnee words. But he had the most unusual way of putting them together. And he had the kindest eyes the boy had ever seen.

"What is your name, sir?" See-a-way asked, biting his tongue for fear the stranger would think him brazen and stop talking.

"El-e-ney Squaw-thee Scoo-tee," the man said with a very broad smile.

It was a most unusual name. It meant Man of Little Fire. For such a large person to be named *little* anything was humorous. The boy should not have laughed, he knew that, for to do so was certainly improper. He was sure he would not have, if the man had not smiled first.

"Have you come to live with us, Man of Little Fire?"

"I expect to live among your people for a long, long time, See-a-way," he said.

"Did you know any white men, where you came from?"

"I knew them to some extent," he said. The boy trembled as he imagined how many white men this strange tall Indian might have killed in his life.

"My father who has died," the boy said bitterly, "was going to assign me a wild turkey for my manhood hunt. But I hope my new father will assign me a white man to shoot. It should make for a hunt of great skill and danger, don't you think?"

See-a-way held his breath, waiting for the answer.

"I think," the stranger said, "that you must hunt whatever your father tells you to hunt, Ka-an-ah See-a-way."

The boy could not be sure whether that meant he was for the idea or not. Everything he said was strange. The boy looked up into his eyes. Even they were a strange color. They contained some of the sky and some clear creek water and little spots from the breast of a wild chicken.

"Are you a Shawnee, Man of Little Fire?"

"I am your brother and your friend," he said, lifting his hand in farewell.

See-a-way's new father, Buffalo Man, was one of the most honorable Shawnees in the community. He had a daughter and two sons, all younger than See-a-way. His wife had died on the journey from Kansas into the Indian Territory. A rattlesnake bite and a fever in the rain could not be cured by the herb medicine she was given.

See-a-way pretended to be very happy with his mother's decision. That was expected of him. And there was certainly nothing wrong with Buffalo Man. Indeed, he was a lucky boy, for Buffalo Man would be very good to him. It would be disrespectful to wish that his own father were still with him, but if he could have allowed himself to make a wish, that's what he would have wished. . . . So he did not let himself think about his father at all.

The Stained Heart

Now the Shawnees and Pottawatomies were even with each other in the horse-stealing raids, and See-a-way hoped no further warfare would break out between them. He did not think seriously about going on the warpath like a wild Indian of the plains until after he left the *we-gi-wa* of his sister and Wis-ke-lu-tha.

They lived in the valley between the boy's own *we-gi-wa* and the creek, at the bottom of the green grass hill. Every day, while he was living with them, he sat on a high stone ledge near the creek and pretended to be scouting for his people. He would sit very still for hours, watching for any white man who might approach the Shawnee community. He would imagine that he saw one, creeping silently through the woods along the creek, and he would jump from the ledge and alert his people just in time to save them. Everyone would think it was marvelous that a boy who had not yet reached his manhood could be such a hero, and he would be pronounced a man by special proclamation of the Shawnee chief.

One day Wis-ke-lu-tha took him for a walk—a very unusual thing for him to do.

The boy waited for his sister's husband to speak. But Wis-ke-lu-tha quietly watched, for a long while, as the boy practiced shooting at wild chickens in the grassland beyond the hillside.

At last Wis-ke-lu-tha spoke. "See-a-way, it is now time for you to go back home to your own *we-gi-wa*. Your new father is gathering his family together. His own daughter and his two young sons will be brought there today. I will take you there and tell him how well you have behaved. I will tell him you are learning to shoot wild chickens with great accuracy. From now on, you will be Buffalo Man's dutiful son."

The boy was disappointed and he did not answer. There was nothing for him to say. He would much rather have stayed with Wis-ke-lu-tha and his sister, where the new lamp made a miracle of the night—but of course he could not. He knew that.

"You will be happy with new brothers and a little sister to play with," Wis-ke-lu-tha told him. "You are very lucky."

"Did you see the white men who killed my

father?" the boy asked. "You were riding near him when he fell...."

Wis-ke-lu-tha looked at him sideways as they walked together. "See-a-way, you should not think about this thing too much."

"Were all the cowboys white men?" the boy persisted. He knew that Indians were sometimes cowboys, but he did not believe that another Indian would have shot his father.

"I am going to tell you something, See-a-way," Wis-ke-lu-tha said, suddenly angry. "You were not supposed to be there on the cattle trail that day! It is not meant for young boys who have not yet reached their manhood to be with men when they are doing things that only men should do!"

"I wanted to see a white man with my own eyes!" the boy cried. "I had never seen one, yet they have caused all the trouble of our people!"

Of course, he should not have tried to justify his actions. That was not proper for a Shawnee boy. It was assumed that an older person would know why a boy did the things he did. Yet See-a-way could not keep from saying what he said.

Wis-ke-lu-tha stopped walking and turned around. He put his hands on his hips, as Blue Eagle had once done; his eyes narrowed into turtle's eyes and his nostrils flared.

"See-a-way! If you had reached your manhood

before you saw this thing you would have been prepared for whatever happened. Do you understand? Now that you have slipped away disobediently and joined the work of men, you have seen something no boy should see. It has stained you with unhappiness that may never go away. If a young boy's heart is stained before he has become a man, he can never be a good Shawnee. Do you realize that your own father would have taken the la-la-so-waw-ka to your legs if he had known what you did?"

The boy trembled but he did not answer. He knew it was true. He looked down at his feet in shame.

"Do you listen to me, See-a-way?" Wis-ke-lu-tha said, shaking the boy's shoulders.

"Yes, I am listening."

"I will return you to your own *we-gi-wa*. I will watch you closely for good behavior. I do not think your new father will assign your next endurance test until he talks to me about it. When both of us agree that you are worthy, you will get it. Not before. Remember that good behavior always includes having proper thoughts. Your actions reflect your thoughts and your thoughts reflect your heart. You must get rid of your anger, or at least learn to control it, or you can never become a man."

Again the boy did not answer.

But it was true. No properly trained Indian, whatever his tribe, would show his feelings about anything unless he wanted to.

"In a little while," said Wis-ke-lu-tha as they walked back slowly, "the new Quaker school will be finished near the agency. It would show me that you were having good thoughts if you went to your new father and told him that you would like to attend the school. Many Shawnee children are going to attend it as soon as possible."

The boy could not answer. He knew that Wis-ke-lu-tha was troubled about him; and for Wis-ke-lu-tha's sake he tried to calm the rage that stormed and stained his heart—but he could not.

Although he did not want to be disrespectful to his new father, he did not really care whether he would ever be given another endurance test or not. The tests, and even his manhood hunt, would never seem important if his own father could not give them.

Tears threatened the boy's eyes. He felt sorry for Wis-ke-lu-tha for having a wife whose little brother was afflicted with such a stain in his heart. But he could not help it. White men had killed his father and cheated the Indians of their land. He could not accept it. He would go on the warpath alone. He didn't care if he were caught or even killed.

The Warpath

WHEN See-a-way realized beyond any doubt that he was going to go on the warpath, he gave up all other interests. His mind was absorbed with trying to plan the most effective way to strike at the white man. He grew so quiet that Wis-ke-lu-tha and his new father were happy with him. They even gave him another endurance test to perform.

He performed it without any great interest because he could not concentrate on anything except his warpath plan.

Always, as he worked on his plan, one central thing came back to him. He was like a grasshopper quietly facing the snake's tongue. There was no escape. No matter what he did, no matter how he behaved, he was facing the Quaker school. And that gave his idea its final shape. . . .

He hurried down to the river at daybreak one morning. The river was rushing muddy-red and high after several days of rain. He swam with all his might to get across, and once he wondered if he had not been foolish to enter such treacherous water.

When he reached the other bank he hurried up through the willows and wild plum thickets to the flat grassland. He took off his clothes and wrung them as dry as he could, then put them back on. He ran up the cattle trail to the point in a hollow a mile or two below the agency. It was a long way to run—more than six miles—which was the distance everyone expected him to go twice each day. For this was the site of the school.

He climbed to the top of the tallest pecan tree in the copse and watched with squinted eyes as the workmen made the building out of the great oak logs. They did not seem to be white men, and he wondered where they could find Indians who were willing to build a school.

His plan was now ready for final action. He went home late in the morning, knowing exactly what he was going to do, and his heart was bursting with excitement.

"See-a-way," said Buffalo Man when he arrived, "I am proud of your last endurance test. I have told Wis-ke-lu-tha that I am proud. We have decided that you deserve another one... See-a-way, are you listening to me?"

"Oh yes, sir," he said, although actually he was not. He had come home for a specific purpose, and he was impatient to continue his plan. He did not intend to lie to his new father, however. He said what he did because he hated to show disrespect by admitting that he had not been listening.

"You are wet. Have you been playing in the creek?"

The boy nodded, hoping he would not be asked any more.

"What have I just been saying to you?" Buffalo Man demanded.

"Something . . . about Wis-ke-lu-tha, sir," the boy said.

His heart was pounding. Telling a lie warranted punishment with the *la-la-so-waw-ka*, but he did not know whether this lie was quite bad enough for that.

With a grunt of disgust, Buffalo Man raised his head as high as his backbone would let it go. He stuck his chin out toward the boy, and folded his huge hands across his chest. See-a-way had always marveled at how big Buffalo Man's hands were.

"I am offering to give you another endurance test if you are ready," he said.

"I am ready, sir," said the boy quickly, although he really was not, for he did not have time right now. But he dared not refuse.

"The river is up," said Buffalo Man. "Go as fast as you can and swim across it and back. Swim strongly—and very carefully—for the river is dangerous."

"I will!" the boy said. Buffalo Man did not know that he had already swum the river twice that day . . . nor that his plan called for him to swim it again!

He ran out and down the hillside. When he neared his sister's *we-gi-wa* he crept silently, watching to see whether his sister was in sight. Wis-ke-lu-tha was on a two-day hunt and would not be there to interfere.

At last, in the high corn, See-a-way caught sight of his sister working a row far ahead of him. Her head was just about even with the tassels.

He knew that he was safe. Hurriedly he entered her *we-gi-wa* and went to the wall peg where Wis-ke-lu-tha kept his *pou-ta-la*.

The Shawnee *pou-ta-la* were originally skins for carrying bear oil, but they did not keep bear oil in them very much any more, for there were very few bears. Nowadays, when they had any money, they could buy coal oil at the trading post. Wis-ke-lu-tha kept coal oil in his *pou-ta-la* for the new lamp.

The boy took the *pou-ta-la* from the peg, and swiftly made his way outside and down the creek to the river.

At the river bank he pulled off his clothes, hanging them on a grapevine in a dense thicket

68

where they would not be seen until he returned.... if he ever did! He took a breechclout from the pocket of his pants. He had secretly made it out of a piece of goatskin during the past few days. He tied it around his waist, stuck his hunting knife inside the strings, slung the *pou-ta-la* over his shoulder again, picked up the rawhide laces with which he normally tied his coatsleeve leggings on, and plunged into the river. He swam with all his might toward the opposite bank.

When he reached the other side he began looking for pokeberries with which to paint stripes on his face and chest. He found them before he reached the cattle trail and gathered a large handful. As he did not want to be seen yet, he went toward the school as fast as he could, keeping to the woods or in the high grass near the trail. When he came to a small creek of clear water, he stopped and looked at his reflection in a pool.

Then he painted stripes on his face with the red berry juice. He found some white clay with which he made white stripes across the red ones from his cheeks to his arms and over his forehead. He painted his ribs alternately red and white.

"See-a-way," he said to his reflection, "you are now a savage Indian of the plains. You can do whatever you want to the white man!"

He smiled with satisfaction. It felt good to look like an Indian—and he realized that wearing homespun clothes was making all the Indians look too much like the white man. He vowed never again to wear anything except the skins of otter, beaver, buffalo, deer and skunk. The pool was a good mirror. He could even see his teeth when he smiled, and he wished he had time to sharpen them—but of course he did not.

Still careful to travel where he would not be seen, he hurried on toward the school.

When he reached the copse in the big hollow, late in the afternoon, he again climbed high into his lookout tree. He could see no one, and knew his luck was good. As though to prove how good it was, when he climbed down from the tree he found a turkey feather on the ground nearby. He tied one of the rawhide laces around his head and stuck the feather in it, exactly as he would after he became a man. It made him feel terribly strange . . . but wonderful!

Then he crept to the schoolhouse. He walked around it, throwing the coal oil from Wis-ke-lu-tha's *pou-ta-la* over the logs, soaking the base of them well. He used every drop of the oil, because he wanted a really big fire.

He went back into the copse and cut a stick with which he would make a firebow out of the other lace from his legging. He found a piece of dry dead log and whittled a flat place on it. He gathered dry grass and a pile of leaves for tinder. Then he rigged up the firebow and spun the spindle into the log until he could see smoke.

Now his heart was beating like a tom-tom!

He worked the bow as fast as he could. The smoke got thicker. Finally it blazed. Quickly he pushed the grass and leaves into the flame and began to blow on it carefully. Soon he had a nice small fire going beside the log.

By the time he had gathered some pitch pine knots it was almost dark. Now he was ready. He did a little war dance around his fire, whooped as loud as he could with the war cry of the Comanche, set two pine knots ablaze, and listened with satisfaction to the sizzling pitch.

He whooped again, this time in the manner of the wild Apache, and ran toward the nearly finished school that he hated.

He flung the torches at the school, first on one side, then on the other—whooping as he danced around the building. He ran back to his fire in the copse and lit two more torches. Yelling wildly, he ran and threw them at the other two sides of the school.

The fire was catching beautifully. As he whooped and danced around, it began to send up a wonderful blaze in the early darkness.

Once more he ran back to his fire and lit two

more pine knots. Already he could hear voices. The fire had been seen, but it was too late for them to stop it now. His warpath had done its most important work!

People were approaching. He waited for them, dancing again around the burning building with his torches. He was ready to throw the flaming knots at the first white face he saw.

Then he heard someone shout, "It's a wild Indian from the plains!"

In the same instant he heard the twang of a longbow string.

An arrow hit his thigh, striking numbness into his body, and he fell to the ground.

And then Blue Eagle was standing over him with a longbow in his hand.

"Blue Eagle," the boy said, "it is me! See-a-way, your Shawnee friend!"

"I know who it is," Blue Eagle said. "I watched you swim across the river, and I watched you paint your face. You are as stupid as all the sheep and all the cows put together."

"I decided to go on the warpath against the white man," the boy said.

"You sure went through the woods fast, See-a-way. I lost you completely, and decided you must be going to burn the agency. So I went there first, or I would never have let you get this far with your foolish warpath. Don't you know they will simply build another school? Come—hurry into the woods. I will hide you before they find us. They might shoot you, with all that war paint on. White men get excited very easily. . . ."

Again the boy heard the voices, coming closer. He tried to get up to go with Blue Eagle, but his leg buckled under him. His hip and thigh were no longer numb. They were throbbing with pain.

"I don't think I can walk," he said. "Why did you shoot me?"

"I had to, to make you stop," Blue Eagle said, picking the boy up in his arms and running deep into the woods, away from the burning school. "I'm always having to save you," he said with disgust in his voice.

Before they traveled very far into the woods, the boy felt everything go black. The last thing he remembered was the sound of angry voices back at the school.

And he thought with a sigh that at least he had destroyed the school. That was worth anything that might happen to him now. He would certainly feel the *la-la-so-waw-ka* later—but he did not care.

The Rawhide Face

HE REMEMBERED how he felt just before he opened his eyes. His mind swam toward consciousness with the frantic urge to get there—in much the same way that he had swum the swollen muddy-red river. His eyes opened, and he realized that he had been almost aware of things around him for quite some time.

He was lying on a table. He remembered that he had been wounded by Blue Eagle's arrow and carried by Blue Eagle to safety.

Straining to clear his vision, the boy was astonished to discover that he was looking not at Blue Eagle but at Man of Little Fire whose rawhide face and large black hat had so impressed him during the mourning for his father.

"Hello, See-a-way," the man said with a smile that crinkled the rawhide skin around his eyes. The boy noticed that the eyes still had some blue sky and some clear creek water in them; and he realized, too, that he was inside a cabin where a coal oil lamp flickered against log walls.

"Hello, El-e-ney Squaw-thee Scoo-tee," the boy said.

"How do you feel?"

"Just fine." The boy marveled, as he had before, at the strange way Man of Little Fire spoke the Shawnee language. "I destroyed the white man's school. Now he cannot flick his tongue at me!" he added with pride.

"Does your leg hurt much?"

"Not much," he said. "Did Blue Eagle bring me from the woods into your cabin?"

"Yes. And he is still here."

The boy looked around the cabin, which was a fine one—exactly the kind he had hoped his own family might live in some day. He saw Blue Eagle, standing with arms folded, frowning down at him.

"My arrow broke off in your thigh," Blue Eagle said. "It will have to be cut out."

"My father cut a *kaw-qua* quill out of my hand for my second endurance test. It did not hurt," the boy said.

Man of Little Fire leaned over and touched his shoulder. "See-a-way, I am glad you have completed that part of your endurance tests. There is no doctor near us, and I think I will let Blue Eagle take the arrow out of your leg. I will hold your hand—"

"You don't need to," the boy said quickly.

"Very well. Let's see if you can lie perfectly still, See-a-way."

He did not even let a nostril quiver. It was a good thing his father had given him the *kaw-qua* quill test, for he knew now that he could force his mind to think away from the pain, and therefore the pain would be helpless to hurt him. He let pictures of the burning school play in his mind, because that was the happiest thing that had happened since the day he moved into his mother's new *we-gi-wa* after the long journey from Kansas.

Or perhaps since the day Wis-ke-lu-tha gave the coal oil lamp to his sister for their marriage. He felt sorry about Wis-ke-lu-tha's *pou-ta-la*. He could not remember what had happened to it after he had poured all the oil out of it. In the excitement of his war dance, he had probably left it somewhere in the woods near the fire. He hoped it had not been burned.

He was very glad when Blue Eagle got the arrow out and poured over the wound something from a bottle which Man of Little Fire handed him.

Blue Eagle said, when he stepped back at last, "I wish I had not been forced to shoot you. If my aim had been bad, I might have killed you, and then my people would have scorned me for killing a boy who had not even reached his manhood. See-a-way, you will have to become clever like a panther, not stupid like a sheep, before you can ever pass your manhood hunt."

"I am glad you were the one who shot me, Blue Eagle, for I have seen what a good shot you are with your longbow," the boy said. "Now that the school has been destroyed, we are all safe from the white man's tongue."

"But it was *not* destroyed."

The boy could not imagine what Blue Eagle meant. He had seen the school going up in flames. Once more Blue Eagle crossed his arms on his chest and shook his head as he stood staring down.

The boy glanced toward Man of Little Fire. He too was shaking his head.

"See-a-way," he said, "you might have known that green oak logs will not burn easily. All that burned was the coal oil that you poured on the schoolhouse. You only blackened those logs a little bit—you did not burn them at all. And a sod roof would never burn. . . ."

Disappointment was so great that he wanted to cry. But he could not do such a thing in the presence of Blue Eagle. Not only would it have reflected discredit on his own people, it would have disgraced him among all the Pottawatomie.

And it would have disgraced Blue Eagle for having befriended such a boy.

"I will go on the warpath again!" he said. "I will strike at the white men once more, as soon as I can! I hate them—all of them!"

Man of Little Fire turned away and went outside the cabin.

Blue Eagle looked down at the boy; and, shaking his head more in anger than sadness, said, "Tell me why you hate El-e-ney Squaw-thee Scoo-tee. He has befriended you by letting me bring you into his cabin. He has refused to tell his people who tried to burn his school."

"His . . . people?" the boy asked. "Is he a—?"

"He is a white man, See-a-way. Oh, you are not at all like the cat or the fox, are you? You are not even like the beaver!"

"But . . . he is not white! He is the color of rawhide."

"He is the color of white men who stay in the sunshine. You do not know anything, do you? I guess I will have to teach you a lot, or you will be getting into trouble the rest of your life, and I will be kept busy saving you."

Blue Eagle stood as stiff as a totem pole, except for his head, which he shook without hope as he looked down.

Soon Man of Little Fire came back inside the

cabin. His eyes still had the sky and the creek in them, for which the boy was thankful—he didn't know why. His heart pounded when he looked at the rawhide face—the first time he had ever realized that he was looking at a white man.

"See-a-way," said the man after a moment, "I must apologize. I did not tell you, at your father's mourning, that I was a white man. I knew at the time that you were deceived . . . and I am ashamed."

"I thought you were a strange Shawnee," said the boy. "Are you the . . . Quaker schoolmaster my father told me about?"

Man of Little Fire nodded his head and his face broke into a smile. For a while they looked at each other, but the boy did not smile.

Then the "strange Indian" explained that in the English language his name was Sparkman, and that a spark was a very small fire, like that produced by striking flint against steel.

The boy lay very still on the table, listening. He did not know what to say. He could not hate El-e-ney Squaw-thee Scoo-tee as much as he wanted to. He had come to respect a white man without knowing it. He had been fooled. Of course, the man was not as white as he had always thought white men were. He had thought they were the color of clouds, or the white tips of turkey feathers—or the tails of deer.

"See-a-way," El-e-ney Squaw-thee Scoo-tee finally said, as the boy stared up at the rafter poles of the fine cabin, "I hope that you will remember this one thing. Regardless of whatever you decide to think of me."

"What is that?" the boy asked.

"Remember always that I am your friend."

The boy did not answer. He did not want a white man for a friend.

He closed his eyes and lay in silence. Finally he fell asleep for a while, and when he woke the cabin was in darkness except for a brilliant moonstream from the window and the open door.

He was still lying on the table. A light blanket had been thrown over him and he felt much too hot under it. He pushed it aside and sat up painfully on the edge of the table.

In the moonstream he could see Man of Little Fire lying asleep on his bed.

See-a-way lowered himself carefully to the floor. He walked with difficulty to the doorway, prepared to run into the woods. His wound was so painful he wondered if he could find the strength to run. Then he heard the Quaker's voice behind him.

"I left the door open, See-a-way . . . so that you could leave if you wanted to."

The boy's blood pounded, and after a moment he heard the Quaker continue:

"I will keep the door open—at least until cold weather comes—in case you might like to return for a visit."

"Where is Blue Eagle?" the boy asked.

"He went home soon after you fell asleep."

"I would like to go home," said the boy, "but I don't think I can make it yet."

"Perhaps you will stay with me a few days—until you feel like traveling such a long way. I would like you to take my bed, See-a-way . . . perhaps it is big enough for both of us."

"No . . ." said the boy in bitter confusion. "I will sleep on the table."

He hobbled back and climbed onto the table again. Sweat poured from his face and he breathed hard. He suddenly felt chilled and reached to pull the blanket over him, but Man of Little Fire was at his side instantly, covering him.

"You must not catch cold, See-a-way. . . ."

The boy trembled. How could he hate someone who was so kind to him? He knew he could not, and the knowledge caused him to weep silently in the dark night.

Rabbit Snares

DURING the days he spent back at home in his mother's *we-gi-wa*, waiting for his wound to heal, the boy thought about his white *ka-an-ah* who had the sky and creek water in his eyes and also specks from the breast of a wild chicken. And he realized soon that his new father, Buffalo Man, had no intention of punishing him.

He was sure that the Quaker schoolmaster had not told a lie to Buffalo Man and his mother. The Quaker would never have told them anything except the truth. But the boy was very puzzled. His attempt to go on the warpath was certainly sufficient cause for someone to use the *la-la-so-waw-ka* on him. When no one did, his conscience hurt him so much that he made up his mind to use the *la-la-so-waw-ka* on himself. He could not feel right without a proper punishment.

He decided to take it to his right leg, because his left one still suffered from the injury caused by Blue Eagle's arrow.

He went alone into the woods, took off his

leggings, pulled up his pants and scratched his leg deeply, again and again. The *la-la-so-waw-ka* thorns hurt much more than Blue Eagle's arrow had hurt, but the boy felt strangely better after he had done it.

Shortly afterward his new father said, "See-a-way, I believe you have given yourself a punishment." He had seen the scratched leg.

"I have," the boy admitted.

"Your conduct must have been very bad. What did you do besides try to burn the school?"

"I painted my face and went on the warpath." The boy looked at the ground. "But that is not the worst part. The worst thing I did was to wear a turkey feather for a while and pretend to be a man."

"It is no wonder you decided you needed the *la-la-so-waw-ka*. I don't blame you for doing what you did to yourself. You deserved the punishment." Buffalo Man paused, looked at the boy thoughtfully for a moment, then said, "I believe your wounded leg has recovered, hasn't it?"

"Almost," the boy replied.

"Our *ka-an-ah* from the school has reported to me that you lay perfectly still and let the arrow be cut out. He said you performed with a very fine endurance."

The boy was silent, but he was pleased.

"Our *ka-an-ah* asked me to let him give you an endurance test," said Buffalo Man. "On the first day you feel strong enough, you may go as fast as you can to his cabin. His door will be open in case you decide to go there. He will give you your next test. If you do not want to go, I will give you your next test when I think you are ready for it."

The boy ran that very afternoon. For it was perfectly obvious that Buffalo Man would wait a long time to give him his next test if he did not go!

Man of Little Fire smiled when he stopped before the open door of the cabin.

"I have come to be given my next endurance test," said the boy.

The Quaker nodded. "Do you remember the tall pecan tree from which you told me you once watched the schoolhouse being built?"

"I do."

"Three days from now, just as the sun is above the horizon, go there and climb up into the very top of that tree. You will find something that may surprise you. Stay up in the tree until you hear someone calling for you to come down. You may have to stay in the tree a long time, so be prepared. I have heard of people having to remain in a tree all day long when they were on sentry duty."

"I will be prepared," said the boy, vastly relieved that the test was something he did not mind doing. He had feared it might be connected with the school.

Three days later, exactly as instructed, he was at the pecan grove. His new father gave him permission to ride a pony, so he went fast along the cattle trail at daybreak, hurrying to reach the grove before the sun could reach the horizon.

When he hobbled the pony at the base of the tree and looked up, he could see something hanging in the top. And when he climbed up to it, he saw Wis-ke-lu-tha's *pou-ta-la*. It was filled with oil.

He waited in the treetop, wondering when he would hear a voice telling him to come down. He waited a long time. Then he heard voices gathering at the schoolhouse.

As he watched, he saw a group of boys playing games in the yard beside the school. They were taking turns throwing a ball, and when one of them threw it very far, the others cheered. He was sure he could throw a ball that far—but of course he would not have wanted to go there to prove it. After the ball game the boys did some wrestling, and then they played jump-frog.

See-a-way watched from the treetop until they all went inside. Soon he saw friend Sparkman coming toward the copse.

If the Quaker tried to trick him into going to

the school, he would jump on his pony and head for the cattle trail so fast no one would know what had happened!

Before the Quaker reached the tree, the boy heard him calling.

"See-a-way . . . can you hear me, my son?"

"Yes," the boy answered from the tree. "I found Wis-ke-lu-tha's *pou-ta-la*."

He stood in the treetop, suddenly hating the Quaker for trying to trick him with an endurance test and calling him son. He waited for the Quaker to instruct him to come inside the school. . . .

"Good! Now, See-a-way, you can come down whenever you want to. Some time during the day you are to return the *pou-ta-la* to the wall peg from which you first took it. That is all!"

"Do you mean . . . that I should return it now?" the boy shouted.

"Whenever you want to. It does not matter, so long as it is returned before the moon is high tonight. I have no time to talk now, See-a-way, because we are going to make some rabbit snares this morning. And at the noon recess we will all be very busy playing ball. Goodbye!"

The Quaker turned and went back to the school as the boy watched from the treetop.

He was so surprised not to have been tricked, that he stayed up in the tree all morning. He pretended to be a sentry and stood perfectly still. Only the breeze swaying the tree could move him. And at noon he watched the boys play ball on the ground beside the school.

Still he stayed in the tree . . . but during the early afternoon he began to wonder what kind of rabbit snares they were making. And soon he climbed slowly down from the tree and took his pony to the grass at the edge of the copse, hobbling him so that he could graze.

Then he crept toward the schoolhouse door to see if he could peer inside.

The door was wide open, and before he knew it he had walked into the room.

He stood for a moment, looking. Blue Eagle was there. And some Kickapoo and Iowa boys. Nobody saw him at first—then Friend Sparkman looked up from the workbench where he was cutting a notch into a stick.

"Here is See-a-way," he said. "Maybe he can tell us something about snares. See-a-way, do you know how to make good rabbit snares?"

"I know how to make a stork-leg snare for rabbits," he said walking hesitantly toward the bench. He would not look at Blue Eagle. He knew how dumb like a sheep or a cow Blue Eagle thought he was.

His heart pounded furiously, but it was not an angry fury. It was more like excitement . . . mixed with a desperate hope that Blue Eagle would not tell everyone what he knew about the Shawnee boy whose foot had slipped on his very first endurance test.

When he reached the bench, Friend Sparkman looked at him. He knew that the Quaker's heart was gentle, and he knew that if he could gentle his own heart, he might yet be assigned to his manhood hunt . . . and pass it. "This is the way to make a stork-leg snare . . ." he said.

He realized, in a curious half-knowing way, that all the boys in the school were as familiar as he with stork-leg rabbit snares. They, as well as the Quaker schoolmaster, were letting him ease his way into sharing their new experience.

The awkwardness of being there began to disappear when the schoolmaster, at last turning from the woodcraft table, said: "Now, let's recite the words of English that we learned this morning."

Suddenly all the boys were alert.

"Tee-qua," the Quaker said. "What is the English word for *tee-qua?*"

"Gun," cried a Shawnee boy who lived near See-a-way above the river.

"Very good," said the schoolmaster. "Who can tell me the English word for *thee-pee?*"

"River!" cried another boy.

"Correct," said the schoolmaster. "Now . . . who can tell me this one? *Sa-cou-ka.*"

"A flintstone," said Blue Eagle.

"That's right, Blue Eagle. Do you also know the English word for *scou-te-ca-ga?*"

"Scou-te-ca-ga means a steel for striking a flintstone," Blue Eagle answered, looking at See-a-way who was excited because he had begun to understand.

Even as the faint glimmer of what was coming next reached him, the schoolmaster said: "See-a-way, can you tell me the English word for *scoo-tee?*"

"Fire!" See-a-way said, delighted.

"And *squaw-thee?*"

"Little!" cried the boy.

"And can you tell the class what a 'little fire' means in English?"

"A spark!" said the boy, smiling broadly. "You taught me that at your cabin."

"Now . . ." said the Quaker, turning deliberately from See-a-way to another boy. "Do you remember the English word for *el-e-ney*?"

"Man," said the boy.

"Very good. If I tell you that my name is El-e-ney Squaw-thee Scoo-tee, what does it mean in English?"

"Man of Little Fire," said the boy.

"No!" cried See-a-way, unable to hold back his rushing comprehension. "It means Sparkman! Doesn't it, sir?"

"Yes, that is correct," said the Quaker, and the look he gave See-a-way was as warm as the sunshine that made the grass and corn and pumpkins grow.

The boy was comforted. He had learned, as his father had told him he must learn, that some white men, if not all of them, could understand the stain in the heart of a young boy who was not white.

See-a-way looked across the room at Blue Eagle. They smiled at each other. They would continue to be friends, he knew . . . and they would continue to learn as much as they could, to help their people.

author's

note

This story of a Shawnee Indian boy's view of the end of the age of the American Indian does not depict the actual life incidents of any person living or dead. All the episodes and characters are imaginary.

For the ritual meaning of "Our Grandmother" and other ceremonial forms and customs the author is indebted to *Shawnee Female Deity* by Charles F. Voeglin from the Yale Publications in Anthropology and to *Civilization* by Thomas Wildcat Alford as told to Florence Drake.

Such a story might actually have happened in the 1870s. It was during this period that western expansion overran the Indian Territory (now the State of Oklahoma) where dozens of Indian tribes from the South, East and North of the United States had already been pushed by the white man. It was here that railroads, and consequently commerce, finally caught up with the American frontier.

And it was here that the Indians of the United States had their destinies established: they could become assimilated into the white man's civilization, or they could remain isolated on their reservations forever.